LITTLE WOMEN

Louisa May Alcott

VOLUME FOUR

Chapters 14-19

first published in 1868

CHAPTER FOURTEEN

SECRETS

Jo was very busy in the garret, for the October days began to grow chilly, and the afternoons were short. For two or three hours the sun lay warmly in the high window, showing Jo seated on the old sofa, writing busily, with her papers spread out upon a trunk before her, while Scrabble, the pet rat, promenaded the beams overhead, accompanied by his oldest son, a fine young fellow, who was evidently very proud of his whiskers. Quite absorbed in her work, Jo scribbled away till the last page was filled, when she signed her name with a flourish and threw down her pen, exclaiming...

"There, I've done my best! If this won't suit I shall have to wait till I can do better."

Lying back on the sofa, she read the manuscript carefully through, making dashes here and there, and putting in many exclamation points, which looked like little balloons.

Then she tied it up with a smart red ribbon, and sat a minute looking at it with a sober, wistful expression, which plainly showed how earnest her work had been. Jo's desk up here was an old tin kitchen which hung against the wall. In it she kept her papers, and a few books, safely shut away from Scrabble, who, being likewise of a literary turn, was fond of making a circulating library of such books as were left in his way by eating the leaves. From this tin receptacle Jo produced another manuscript, and putting both in her pocket, crept quietly downstairs, leaving her friends to nibble on her pens and taste her ink.

She put on her hat and jacket as noiselessly as possible, and going to the back entry window, got out upon the roof of a low porch, swung herself down to the grassy bank, and took a roundabout way to the road. Once there, she composed herself, hailed a passing omnibus, and rolled away to town, looking very merry and mysterious.

If anyone had been watching her, he would have thought her movements decidedly peculiar, for on alighting, she went off at a great pace till she reached a certain number in a certain busy street. Having found the place with some difficulty, she went into the doorway, looked up the dirty stairs, and after standing stock still a minute, suddenly dived into the street and walked away as rapidly as she came. This maneuver she repeated several times, to the great amusement of a black-eyed young gentleman lounging in the window of a building opposite.

On returning for the third time, Jo gave herself a shake, pulled her hat over her eyes, and walked up the stairs, looking as if she were going to have all her teeth out.

There was a dentist's sign, among others, which adorned the entrance, and after staring a moment at the pair of artificial jaws which slowly opened and shut to draw attention to a fine set of teeth, the young gentleman put on his coat, took his hat, and went down to post himself in the opposite doorway, saying with a smile and a shiver, "It's like her to come alone, but if she has a bad time she'll need someone to help her home."

In ten minutes
Jo came running
downstairs with a
very red face and the
general appearance
of a person who had
just passed through a
trying ordeal of some
sort. When she saw
the young gentleman
she looked anything
but pleased, and
passed him with a
nod. But he followed,
asking with an air of
sympathy, "Did you

have a bad time?"

"Not very."

"You got through quickly."

"Yes, thank goodness!"

"Why did you go alone?"

"Didn't want anyone to know."

"You're the oddest fellow I ever saw.

How many did you have out?"

Jo looked at her friend as if she did not understand him, then began to laugh as if mightily amused at something.

"There are two which I want to have come out, but I must wait a week."

"What are you laughing at? You are

up to some mischief, Jo," said Laurie, looking mystified.

"So are you. What were you doing, sir, up in that billiard saloon?"

"Begging your pardon, ma'am, it wasn't a billiard saloon, but a gymnasium, and I was taking a lesson in fencing."

"I'm glad of that."

"Why?"

"You can teach me, and then when we play Hamlet, you can be Laertes, and we'll make a fine thing of the fencing scene."

Laurie burst out with a hearty boy's laugh, which made several passers-by smile in spite of themselves.

"I'll teach you whether we play

Hamlet or not. It's grand fun and will straighten you up capitally. But I don't believe that was your only reason for saying 'I'm glad' in that decided way, was it now?"

"No, I was glad that you were not in the saloon, because I hope you never go to such places. Do you?"

"Not often."

"I wish you wouldn't."

"It's no harm, Jo. I have billiards at home, but it's no fun unless you have good players, so, as I'm fond of it, I come sometimes and have a game with Ned Moffat or some of the other fellows."

"Oh, dear, I'm so sorry, for you'll get to liking it better and better, and will waste time and money, and grow like those dreadful boys. I did hope you'd stay respectable and be a satisfaction to your friends," said Jo, shaking her head.

"Can't a fellow take a little innocent amusement now and then without losing his respectability?" asked Laurie, looking nettled.

"That depends upon how and where he takes it. I don't like Ned and his set, and wish you'd keep out of it. Mother won't let us have him at our house, though he wants to come. And if you grow like him she won't be willing to have us frolic together as we do now."

"Won't she?" asked

Laurie anxiously.

"No, she can't bear fashionable young men, and she'd shut us all up in bandboxes rather than have us associate with them."

"Well, she needn't get out her bandboxes yet. I'm not a fashionable party and don't mean to be, but I do like harmless larks now and then, don't you?"

"Yes, nobody minds them, so lark away, but don't get wild, will you? Or there will be an end of all our good times."

"I'll be a double distilled saint."

"I can't bear saints. Just be a simple, honest, respectable boy, and we'll never desert you. I don't know what I should do if you acted like

Mr. King's son. He had plenty of money, but didn't know how to spend it, and got tipsy and gambled, and ran away, and forged his father's name, I believe, and was altogether horrid."

"You think I'm likely to do the same? Much obliged."

"No, I don't—oh, dear, no!—but I hear

people talking about money being such a temptation, and I sometimes wish you were poor. I shouldn't worry then."

"Do you worry about me, Jo?"

"A little, when you look moody and discontented, as you sometimes do, for you've got such a strong will, if you once get started wrong, I'm afraid it would be hard to stop you."

Laurie walked in silence a few minutes, and Jo watched him, wishing she had held her tongue, for his eyes looked angry, though his lips smiled as if at her warnings.

"Are you going to deliver lectures all the way home?" he asked presently.

"Of course not. Why?"

"Because if you are, I'll take a bus. If you're not, I'd like to walk with you and tell you something very interesting."

"I won't preach any more, and I'd like to hear the news immensely."

"Very well, then, come on. It's a

secret, and if I tell you, you must tell me yours."

"I haven't got any," began Jo, but stopped suddenly, remembering that she had.

"You know you have—you can't hide anything, so up and 'fess, or I won't tell," cried Laurie.

"Is your secret a nice

one?"

"Oh, isn't it! All about people you know, and such fun! You ought to hear it, and I've been aching to tell it this long time. Come, you begin."

"You'll not say anything about it at home, will you?"

"Not a word."

"And you won't tease

me in private?"

"I never tease."

"Yes, you do. You get everything you want out of people. I don't know how you do it, but you are a born wheedler."

"Thank you. Fire away."

"Well, I've left two stories with a newspaperman,

and he's to give his answer next week," whispered Jo, in her confidant's ear.

"Hurrah for Miss March, the celebrated American authoress!" cried Laurie, throwing up his hat and catching it again, to the great delight of two ducks, four cats, five hens, and half a dozen Irish children, for they were out of the city now.

"Hush! It won't come to anything, I dare say, but I couldn't rest till I had tried, and I said nothing about it because I didn't want anyone else to be disappointed."

"It won't fail. Why, Jo, your stories are works of Shakespeare compared to half the rubbish that is published every day. Won't it be fun to see them in print, and shan't we feel proud of our authoress?"

Jo's eyes sparkled, for it is always pleasant to be believed in, and a friend's praise is always sweeter than a dozen newspaper puffs.

"Where's your secret? Play fair,

Teddy, or I'll never believe you again," she said, trying to extinguish the brilliant hopes that blazed up at a word of encouragement.

"I may get into a scrape for telling, but I didn't promise not to, so I will, for I never feel easy in my mind till I've told you any plummy bit of news I get. I know where Meg's glove is."

"Is that all?" said Jo, looking disappointed, as Laurie nodded and twinkled with a face full of mysterious intelligence.

"It's quite enough for the present, as you'll agree when I tell you where it is."

"Tell, then."

Laurie bent, and whispered three words in Jo's ear, which produced a comical change. She stood and stared at him for a minute, looking both surprised and displeased, then walked on, saying sharply, "How do you know?"

"Saw it."

"Where?"

"Pocket."

"All this time?"

"Yes, isn't that romantic?"

"No, it's horrid."

"Don't you like it?"

"Of course I don't. It's ridiculous, it won't be allowed. My patience! What would Meg say?"

"You are not to tell

anyone. Mind that."

"I didn't promise."

"That was understood, and I trusted you."

"Well, I won't for the present, anyway, but I'm disgusted, and wish you hadn't told me."

"I thought you'd be pleased."

"At the idea of

anybody coming to take Meg away? No, thank you."

"You'll feel better about it when somebody comes to take you away."

"I'd like to see anyone try it," cried Jo fiercely.

"So should I!" and Laurie chuckled at the idea.

"I don't think secrets agree with me, I feel rumpled up in my mind since you told me that," said Jo rather ungratefully.

"Race down this hill with me, and you'll be all right," suggested Laurie.

No one was in sight, the smooth road sloped invitingly before her, and finding the temptation irresistible, Jo darted away, soon leaving hat and comb behind her and scattering hairpins as she ran. Laurie reached the goal first and was quite satisfied with the success of his treatment, for his Atlanta came panting up with flying hair, bright eyes, ruddy cheeks, and no signs of dissatisfaction in her face.

"I wish I was a horse, then I could run for miles in this splendid air, and not lose my breath. It was capital, but see what a guy it's made me. Go, pick up my things, like a cherub, as you are," said Jo, dropping down under a maple tree, which was carpeting the bank with crimson leaves.

Laurie leisurely

departed to recover the lost property, and Jo bundled up her braids, hoping no one would pass by till she was tidy again. But someone did pass, and who should it be but Meg, looking particularly ladylike in her state and festival suit, for she had been making calls.

"What in the world

are you doing here?"
she asked, regarding
her disheveled
sister with well-bred
surprise.

"Getting leaves,"
meekly answered
Jo, sorting the rosy
handful she had just
swept up.

"And hairpins," added
Laurie, throwing half
a dozen into Jo's
lap. "They grow on
this road, Meg, so

do combs and brown straw hats."

"You have been running, Jo. How could you? When will you stop such romping ways?" said Meg reprovingly, as she settled her cuffs and smoothed her hair, with which the wind had taken liberties.

"Never till I'm stiff and old and have to

use a crutch. Don't try to make me grow up before my time, Meg. It's hard enough to have you change all of a sudden. Let me be a little girl as long as I can."

As she spoke, Jo bent over the leaves to hide the trembling of her lips, for lately she had felt that Margaret was fast getting to be a woman, and Laurie's secret made her dread the separation which must surely come some time and now seemed very near. He saw the trouble in her face and drew Meg's attention from it by asking quickly, "Where have you been calling, all so fine?"

"At the Gardiners', and Sallie has

been telling me all about Belle Moffat's wedding. It was very splendid, and they have gone to spend the winter in Paris. Just think how delightful that must be!"

"Do you envy her, Meg?" said Laurie.

"I'm afraid I do."

"I'm glad of it!" muttered Jo, tying on

her hat with a jerk.

"Why?" asked Meg, looking surprised.

"Because if you care much about riches, you will never go and marry a poor man," said Jo, frowning at Laurie, who was mutely warning her to mind what she said.

"I shall never 'go and marry' anyone,"

observed Meg, walking on with great dignity while the others followed, laughing, whispering, skipping stones, and 'behaving like children', as Meg said to herself, though she might have been tempted to join them if she had not had her best dress on.

For a week or two, Jo behaved so queerly

that her sisters were quite bewildered. She rushed to the door when the postman rang, was rude to Mr. Brooke whenever they met, would sit looking at Meg with a woe-begone face, occasionally jumping up to shake and then kiss her in a very mysterious manner. Laurie and she were always making signs to one another, and talking about 'Spread Eagles' till the girls declared they had both lost their wits. On the second Saturday after Jo got out of the window, Meg, as she sat sewing at her window, was scandalized by the sight of Laurie chasing Jo all over the garden and finally capturing her in Amy's bower. What went on there, Meg could not see, but shrieks of laughter were heard, followed by the murmur of voices and a great flapping of newspapers.

"What shall we do with that girl? She never will behave like a young lady," sighed Meg, as she watched the race with a disapproving face.

"I hope she won't.

She is so funny and dear as she is," said Beth, who had never betrayed that she was a little hurt at Jo's having secrets with anyone but her.

"It's very trying, but we never can make her commy la fo," added Amy, who sat making some new frills for herself, with her curls tied up in a very becoming way, two agreeable things that made her feel unusually elegant and ladylike.

In a few minutes Jo bounced in, laid herself on the sofa, and affected to read.

"Have you anything interesting there?" asked Meg, with condescension.

"Nothing but a story, won't amount

to much, I guess," returned Jo, carefully keeping the name of the paper out of sight.

"You'd better read it aloud. That will amuse us and keep you out of mischief," said Amy in her most grown-up tone.

"What's the name?" asked Beth, wondering why Jo kept her face behind the sheet.

"The Rival Painters."

"That sounds well. Read it," said Meg.

With a loud "Hem!" and a long breath, Jo began to read very fast. The girls listened with interest, for the tale was romantic, and somewhat pathetic, as most of the characters died in the end. "I like that about the splendid picture," was Amy's approving remark, as Jo paused.

"I prefer the lovering part. Viola and Angelo are two of our favorite names, isn't that queer?" said Meg, wiping her eyes, for the lovering part was tragical.

"Who wrote it?" asked Beth, who had caught a glimpse of

Jo's face.

The reader suddenly sat up, cast away the paper, displaying a flushed countenance, and with a funny mixture of solemnity and excitement replied in a loud voice, "Your sister."

"You?" cried Meg, dropping her work.

"It's very good," said Amy critically.

"I knew it! I knew it! Oh, my Jo, I am so proud!" and Beth ran to hug her sister and exult over this splendid success.

Dear me, how delighted they all were, to be sure! How Meg wouldn't believe it till she saw the words. "Miss Josephine March," actually printed in the paper. How graciously

Amy criticized the artistic parts of the story, and offered hints for a sequel, which unfortunately couldn't be carried out, as the hero and heroine were dead. How Beth got excited, and skipped and sang with joy. How Hannah came in to exclaim, "Sakes alive, well I never!" in great astonishment at 'that Jo's doin's'.

How proud Mrs. March was when she knew it. How Jo laughed, with tears in her eyes, as she declared she might as well be a peacock and done with it, and how the 'Spread Eagle' might be said to flap his wings triumphantly over the House of March, as the paper passed from hand to hand.

"Tell us about it."
"When did it come?"
"How much did you get for it?" "What will Father say?"
"Won't Laurie laugh?" cried the family, all in one breath as they clustered about Jo, for these foolish, affectionate people made a jubilee of every little household joy.

"Stop jabbering,

girls, and I'll tell you everything," said Jo, wondering if Miss Burney felt any grander over her Evelina than she did over her 'Rival Painters'. Having told how she disposed of her tales, Jo added, "And when I went to get my answer, the man said he liked them both, but didn't pay beginners, only let them print in his paper, and noticed the stories. It was good practice, he said, and when the beginners improved, anyone would pay. So I let him have the two stories, and today this was sent to me, and Laurie caught me with it and insisted on seeing it, so I let him. And he said it was good, and I shall write more, and he's going to get the next paid for, and I am so happy, for in time I may be able to support myself and help the girls."

Jo's breath gave out here, and wrapping her head in the paper, she bedewed her little story with a few natural tears, for to be independent and earn the praise of those she loved were the dearest wishes of her heart, and this seemed to be the first step toward that happy end.

CHAPTER FIFTEEN

A TELEGRAM

"November is the most disagreeable month in the whole year," said Margaret, standing at the window one dull afternoon, looking out at the frostbitten garden.

"That's the reason I was born in it," observed Jo

pensively, quite unconscious of the blot on her nose.

"If something very pleasant should happen now, we should think it a delightful month," said Beth, who took a hopeful view of everything, even November.

"I dare say, but nothing pleasant ever does happen in this

family," said Meg, who was out of sorts. "We go grubbing along day after day, without a bit of change, and very little fun. We might as well be in a treadmill."

"My patience, how blue we are!" cried Jo. "I don't much wonder, poor dear, for you see other girls having splendid times, while you grind, grind, year in and year out. Oh, don't I wish I could manage things for you as I do for my heroines! You're pretty enough and good enough already, so I'd have some rich relation leave you a fortune unexpectedly. Then you'd dash out as an heiress, scorn everyone who has slighted you, go abroad, and come home my Lady

Something in a blaze of splendor and elegance."

"People don't have fortunes left them in that style nowadays, men have to work and women marry for money. It's a dreadfully unjust world," said Meg bitterly.

"Jo and I are going to make fortunes for you all. Just wait ten years, and see if we don't," said Amy, who sat in a corner making mud pies, as Hannah called her little clay models of birds, fruit, and faces.

"Can't wait, and I'm afraid I haven't much faith in ink and dirt, though I'm grateful for your good intentions."

Meg sighed, and

turned to the frostbitten garden again. Jo groaned and leaned both elbows on the table in a despondent attitude, but Amy spatted away energetically, and Beth, who sat at the other window, said, smiling, "Two pleasant things are going to happen right away. Marmee is coming down the street, and Laurie is tramping through the garden as if he had something nice to tell."

In they both came, Mrs. March with her usual question, "Any letter from Father, girls?" and Laurie to say in his persuasive way, "Won't some of you come for a drive? I've been working away at mathematics till my head is in a muddle, and I'm going to freshen my wits by a brisk turn. It's a dull day, but the air isn't bad, and I'm going to take Brooke home, so it will be gay inside, if it isn't out. Come, Jo, you and Beth will go, won't you?"

"Of course we will."

"Much obliged, but I'm busy." And Meg whisked out her workbasket, for she had agreed with her mother that it was best, for her at least, not to drive too often with the young gentleman.

"We three will be ready in a minute," cried Amy, running away to wash her hands.

"Can I do anything for you, Madam Mother?" asked Laurie, leaning over

Mrs. March's chair with the affectionate look and tone he always gave her.

"No, thank you, except call at the office, if you'll be so kind, dear. It's our day for a letter, and the postman hasn't been. Father is as regular as the sun, but there's some delay on the way, perhaps."

A sharp ring interrupted her, and a minute after Hannah came in with a letter.

"It's one of them horrid telegraph things, mum," she said, handling it as if she was afraid it would explode and do some damage.

At the word 'telegraph', Mrs. March snatched it, read the two lines it contained, and dropped back into her chair as white as if the little paper had sent a bullet to her heart. Laurie dashed downstairs for water, while Meg and Hannah supported her, and Jo read aloud, in a frightened voice...

Mrs. March:
Your husband is very ill. Come at once.
S. HALE

Blank Hospital, Washington.

How still the room was as they listened breathlessly, how strangely the day darkened outside, and how suddenly the whole world seemed to change, as the girls gathered about their mother, feeling as if all the happiness and support of their lives was about to be taken from them.

Mrs. March was herself again directly, read the message over, and stretched out her arms to her daughters, saying, in a tone they never forgot, "I shall go at once, but it may be too late. Oh, children, children, help me to bear it!"

For several minutes there was nothing

but the sound of sobbing in the room, mingled with broken words of comfort, tender assurances of help, and hopeful whispers that died away in tears. Poor Hannah was the first to recover, and with unconscious wisdom she set all the rest a good example, for with her, work was panacea for most afflictions.

"The Lord keep the dear man! I won't waste no time a-cryin', but git your things ready right away, mum," she said heartily, as she wiped her face on her apron, gave her mistress a warm shake of the hand with her own hard one, and went away to work like three women in one.

"She's right, there's

no time for tears now. Be calm, girls, and let me think."

They tried to be calm, poor things, as their mother sat up, looking pale but steady, and put away her grief to think and plan for them.

"Where's Laurie?" she asked presently, when she had collected her thoughts and decided on the first duties to be done.

"Here, ma'am. Oh, let me do something!" cried the boy, hurrying from the next room whither he had withdrawn, feeling that their first sorrow was too sacred for even his friendly eyes to see.

"Send a telegram saying I will come at once. The next

train goes early in the morning. I'll take that."

"What else? The horses are ready. I can go anywhere, do anything," he said, looking ready to fly to the ends of the earth.

"Leave a note at Aunt March's. Jo, give me that pen and paper."

Tearing off the blank side of one of her newly copied pages, Jo drew the table before her mother, well knowing that money for the long, sad journey must be borrowed, and feeling as if she could do anything to add a little to the sum for her father.

"Now go, dear, but don't kill yourself

driving at a desperate pace. There is no need of that."

Mrs. March's warning was evidently thrown away, for five minutes later Laurie tore by the window on his own fleet horse, riding as if for his life.

"Jo, run to the rooms, and tell Mrs. King that I can't come. On the way get these things. I'll put them down, they'll be needed and I must go prepared for nursing. Hospital stores are not always good. Beth, go and ask Mr. Laurence for a couple of bottles of old wine. I'm not too proud to beg for Father. He shall have the best of everything. Amy, tell Hannah to get down the black trunk, and Meg, come and help me find my things, for I'm half bewildered."

Writing, thinking, and directing all at once might well bewilder the poor lady, and Meg begged her to sit quietly in her room for a little while, and let them work. Everyone scattered like leaves before a gust of wind, and the quiet, happy household was broken up as suddenly as if the paper had been an evil spell.

Mr. Laurence came hurrying back with Beth, bringing every comfort the kind old gentleman could think of for the invalid, and friendliest promises of protection for the girls during the mother's absence, which comforted her very much. There was nothing he didn't offer, from his own dressing gown to himself as escort. But the last was impossible. Mrs. March would not hear of the old gentleman's undertaking the long journey, yet an expression of relief was visible when he spoke of it, for anxiety ill fits one for traveling. He saw the look, knit his heavy eyebrows, rubbed his hands, and marched abruptly away, saying he'd be back directly. No one had time to think of him again till, as Meg ran through the entry, with a pair of rubbers in one hand and a cup of tea in the other, she came suddenly upon Mr. Brooke.

"I'm very sorry to hear of this, Miss March," he said, in the kind, quiet tone which sounded very pleasantly to her perturbed spirit. "I came to offer myself as escort to your mother. Mr. Laurence has commissions for me in Washington, and it will give me real satisfaction to be of service to her there."

Down dropped the rubbers, and the tea was very near following, as Meg put out her hand, with a face so full of gratitude that Mr. Brooke would have felt repaid for a much greater sacrifice than the trifling one of time and comfort which he was about to take.

"How kind you all are!

Mother will accept, I'm sure, and it will be such a relief to know that she has someone to take care of her. Thank you very, very much!"

Meg spoke earnestly, and forgot herself entirely till something in the brown eyes looking down at her made her remember the cooling tea, and lead the way into the parlor, saying she would call her mother.

Everything was arranged by the time Laurie returned with a note from Aunt March, enclosing the desired sum, and a few lines repeating what she had often said before, that she had always told them it was absurd for March to go into the army, always predicted that no good would come of it, and she hoped they would take her advice the next time. Mrs. March put the note in the fire, the money in her purse, and went on with her preparations, with her lips folded tightly in a way which Jo would have understood if she had been there.

The short afternoon

wore away. All other errands were done, and Meg and her mother busy at some necessary needlework, while Beth and Amy got tea, and Hannah finished her ironing with what she called a 'slap and a bang', but still Jo did not come. They began to get anxious, and Laurie went off to find her, for no one knew what freak Jo might take into her head. He missed her, however, and she came walking in with a very queer expression of countenance, for there was a mixture of fun and fear, satisfaction and regret in it, which puzzled the family as much as did the roll of bills she laid before her mother, saying with a little choke in her voice, "That's my contribution toward making Father comfortable and bringing him home!"

"My dear, where did you get it? Twenty-five dollars! Jo, I hope you haven't done anything rash?"

"No, it's mine honestly. I didn't beg, borrow, or steal it. I earned it, and I don't think you'll blame me, for I only sold what was my own."

As she spoke, Jo took off her bonnet, and a general outcry arose, for all her abundant hair was cut short.

"Your hair! Your beautiful hair!" "Oh, Jo, how could you? Your one beauty." "My dear girl, there was no need of this." "She doesn't look like my Jo any more, but I love her dearly for it!"

As everyone exclaimed, and Beth hugged the cropped head tenderly, Jo assumed an indifferent air, which did not deceive anyone a particle, and said, rumpling up the brown bush and trying to look as if she liked it, "It doesn't affect the fate of the nation, so don't wail, Beth. It will be good for my vanity, I was getting too proud of my wig. It will do my brains good to have that mop taken off. My head feels deliciously light and cool, and the barber said I could soon have a curly crop, which will be boyish, becoming, and easy to keep in order. I'm satisfied, so please take the money and let's have supper."

"Tell me all about it, Jo. I am not quite satisfied, but I can't blame you, for I know how willingly you sacrificed your vanity, as you call it, to your love. But, my dear, it was not necessary, and I'm afraid you will regret it one of these days," said Mrs.

March.

"No, I won't!" returned Jo stoutly, feeling much relieved that her prank was not entirely condemned.

"What made you do it?" asked Amy, who would as soon have thought of cutting off her head as her pretty hair.

"Well, I was wild to

do something for Father," replied Jo, as they gathered about the table, for healthy young people can eat even in the midst of trouble. "I hate to borrow as much as Mother does, and I knew Aunt March would croak, she always does, if you ask for a ninepence. Meg gave all her quarterly salary toward the rent, and I only got some clothes with mine, so I felt wicked, and was bound to have some money, if I sold the nose off my face to get it."

"You needn't feel wicked, my child! You had no winter things and got the simplest with your own hard earnings," said Mrs. March with a look that warmed Jo's heart.

"I hadn't the least idea of selling my hair at first, but as I went along I kept thinking what I could do, and feeling as if I'd like to dive into some of the rich stores and help myself. In a barber's window I saw tails of hair with the prices marked, and one black tail, not so thick as mine, was forty dollars. It came to me all of a sudden that I had one thing to make money out of, and without stopping to think, I walked in, asked if they bought hair, and what they would give for mine."

"I don't see how you dared to do it," said Beth in a tone of awe.

"Oh, he was a little

man who looked as if he merely lived to oil his hair. He rather stared at first, as if he wasn't used to having girls bounce into his shop and ask him to buy their hair. He said he didn't care about mine, it wasn't the fashionable color, and he never paid much for it in the first place. The work put into it made it dear, and so on. It

was getting late,
and I was afraid if
it wasn't done right
away that I shouldn't
have it done at all,
and you know when I
start to do a thing, I
hate to give it up. So
I begged him to take
it, and told him why
I was in such a hurry.
It was silly, I dare
say, but it changed
his mind, for I got
rather excited, and
told the story in my

topsy-turvy way, and his wife heard, and said so kindly, 'Take it, Thomas, and oblige the young lady. I'd do as much for our Jimmy any day if I had a spire of hair worth selling."

"Who was Jimmy?" asked Amy, who liked to have things explained as they went along.

"Her son, she said,

who was in the army. How friendly such things make strangers feel, don't they? She talked away all the time the man clipped, and diverted my mind nicely."

"Didn't you feel dreadfully when the first cut came?" asked Meg, with a shiver.

"I took a last look at

my hair while the man got his things, and that was the end of it. I never snivel over trifles like that. I will confess, though, I felt queer when I saw the dear old hair laid out on the table, and felt only the short rough ends of my head. It almost seemed as if I'd an arm or leg off. The woman saw me look at it, and picked out a long lock for me to keep. I'll give it to you, Marmee, just to remember past glories by, for a crop is so comfortable I don't think I shall ever have a mane again."

Mrs. March folded the wavy chestnut lock, and laid it away with a short gray one in her desk. She only said, "Thank you, deary," but something in her face made the girls change the subject, and talk as cheerfully as they could about Mr. Brooke's kindness, the prospect of a fine day tomorrow, and the happy times they would have when Father came home to be nursed.

No one wanted to go to bed when at ten o'clock Mrs. March

put by the last finished job, and said, "Come girls." Beth went to the piano and played the father's favorite hymn. All began bravely, but broke down one by one till Beth was left alone, singing with all her heart, for to her music was always a sweet consoler.

"Go to bed and don't talk, for we must be

up early and shall need all the sleep we can get. Good night, my darlings," said Mrs. March, as the hymn ended, for no one cared to try another.

They kissed her quietly, and went to bed as silently as if the dear invalid lay in the next room. Beth and Amy soon fell asleep in spite of the great trouble, but Meg lay awake, thinking the most serious thoughts she had ever known in her short life. Jo lay motionless, and her sister fancied that she was asleep, till a stifled sob made her exclaim, as she touched a wet cheek...

"Jo, dear, what is it? Are you crying about

father?"

"No, not now."

"What then?"

"My... My hair!" burst out poor Jo, trying vainly to smother her emotion in the pillow.

It did not seem at all comical to Meg, who kissed and caressed the afflicted heroine in the tenderest manner.

"I'm not sorry," protested Jo, with a choke. "I'd do it again tomorrow, if I could. It's only the vain part of me that goes and cries in this silly way. Don't tell anyone, it's all over now. I thought you were asleep, so I just made a little private moan for my one beauty. How came you to be awake?"

"I can't sleep, I'm so anxious," said Meg.

"Think about something pleasant, and you'll soon drop off."

"I tried it, but felt wider awake than ever."

"What did you think of?"

"Handsome faces—eyes particularly,"

answered Meg, smiling to herself in the dark.

"What color do you like best?"

"Brown, that is, sometimes. Blue are lovely."

Jo laughed, and Meg sharply ordered her not to talk, then amiably promised to make her hair curl, and fell asleep to dream of living in her castle in the air.

The clocks were striking midnight and the rooms were very still as a figure glided quietly from bed to bed, smoothing a coverlet here, settling a pillow there, and pausing to look long and tenderly at each unconscious face, to kiss each with lips that mutely blessed, and to pray the fervent prayers which only mothers utter. As she lifted the curtain to look out into the dreary night, the moon broke suddenly from behind the clouds and shone upon her like a bright, benignant face, which seemed to whisper in the silence, "Be comforted, dear soul! There is always light behind the clouds."

CHAPTER SIXTEEN

LETTERS

In the cold gray dawn the sisters lit their lamp and read their chapter with an earnestness never felt before. For now the shadow of a real trouble had come, the little books were full of help and comfort, and as they dressed, they agreed to say goodbye cheerfully and hopefully, and send their mother on her anxious journey unsaddened by tears or complaints from them. Everything seemed very strange when they went down, so dim and still outside, so full of light and bustle within. Breakfast at that early hour seemed odd, and even Hannah's familiar face looked unnatural as she flew about her kitchen with her nightcap on. The big trunk stood ready in the hall, Mother's cloak and bonnet lay on the sofa, and Mother herself sat trying to eat, but looking so pale and worn with sleeplessness and anxiety that the girls found it very hard to keep their resolution. Meg's eyes kept filling in spite of herself, Jo was obliged to hide her face in the kitchen roller more than once, and the little girls wore a grave, troubled expression, as if sorrow was a new experience to them.

Nobody talked much, but as the time drew very near and they sat waiting for the carriage, Mrs. March said to the girls, who were all busied about her, one folding her shawl, another smoothing out the strings of her bonnet, a third putting on her overshoes, and a fourth fastening up her travelling bag...

"Children, I leave you to Hannah's care and Mr. Laurence's protection. Hannah is faithfulness itself, and

our good neighbor
will guard you as if
you were his own.
I have no fears for
you, yet I am anxious
that you should take
this trouble rightly.
Don't grieve and fret
when I am gone, or
think that you can
be idle and comfort
yourselves by being
idle and trying to
forget. Go on with
your work as usual,
for work is a blessed

solace. Hope and keep busy, and whatever happens, remember that you never can be fatherless."

"Yes, Mother."

"Meg, dear, be prudent, watch over your sisters, consult Hannah, and in any perplexity, go to Mr. Laurence. Be patient, Jo, don't get despondent or do rash things, write to me often, and be my brave girl, ready to help and cheer all. Beth, comfort yourself with your music, and be faithful to the little home duties, and you, Amy, help all you can, be obedient, and keep happy safe at home."

"We will, Mother! We will!"

The rattle of an approaching carriage

made them all start
and listen. That was
the hard minute, but
the girls stood it
well. No one cried,
no one ran away or
uttered a lamentation,
though their hearts
were very heavy
as they sent loving
messages to Father,
remembering, as they
spoke that it might
be too late to deliver
them. They kissed
their mother quietly,

clung about her tenderly, and tried to wave their hands cheerfully when she drove away.

Laurie and his grandfather came over to see her off, and Mr. Brooke looked so strong and sensible and kind that the girls christened him 'Mr. Greatheart' on the spot.

"Good-by, my

darlings! God bless and keep us all!" whispered Mrs. March, as she kissed one dear little face after the other, and hurried into the carriage.

As she rolled away, the sun came out, and looking back, she saw it shining on the group at the gate like a good omen. They saw it also, and smiled and waved their hands, and the last thing she beheld as she turned the corner was the four bright faces, and behind them like a bodyguard, old Mr. Laurence, faithful Hannah, and devoted Laurie.

"How kind everyone is to us!" she said, turning to find fresh proof of it in the respectful sympathy of the young man's face.

"I don't see how they can help it," returned Mr. Brooke, laughing so infectiously that Mrs. March could not help smiling. And so the journey began with the good omens of sunshine, smiles, and cheerful words.

"I feel as if there had been an earthquake," said Jo, as their neighbors went home to breakfast, leaving them to rest and refresh themselves.

"It seems as if half the house was gone," added Meg forlornly.

Beth opened her lips to say something, but could only point to the pile of nicely mended hose which lay on Mother's table, showing that even in her last hurried moments she had thought and worked for them. It was a little thing, but it went straight to their hearts, and in spite of their brave resolutions, they all broke down and cried bitterly.

Hannah wisely allowed them to relieve their feelings, and when the shower showed signs of clearing up, she came to the rescue, armed with a coffeepot.

"Now, my dear young ladies, remember what your ma said, and don't fret. Come and have a cup of coffee all round, and then let's fall to work and be a credit to the family."

Coffee was a treat, and Hannah showed great tact in making

it that morning. No one could resist her persuasive nods, or the fragrant invitation issuing from the nose of the coffee pot. They drew up to the table, exchanged their handkerchiefs for napkins, and in ten minutes were all right again.

"'Hope and keep busy', that's the motto for us, so

let's see who will remember it best. I shall go to Aunt March, as usual. Oh, won't she lecture though!" said Jo, as she sipped with returning spirit.

"I shall go to my Kings, though I'd much rather stay at home and attend to things here," said Meg, wishing she hadn't made her eyes so red.

"No need of that. Beth and I can keep house perfectly well," put in Amy, with an important air.

"Hannah will tell us what to do, and we'll have everything nice when you come home," added Beth, getting out her mop and dish tub without delay.

"I think anxiety is very interesting," observed Amy, eating sugar pensively.

The girls couldn't help laughing, and felt better for it, though Meg shook her head at the young lady who could find consolation in a sugar bowl.

The sight of the turnovers made Jo sober again;

and when the two
went out to their
daily tasks, they
looked sorrowfully
back at the window
where they were
accustomed to see
their mother's face.
It was gone, but Beth
had remembered
the little household
ceremony, and there
she was, nodding
away at them like a
rosyfaced mandarin.

"That's so like my Beth!" said Jo, waving her hat, with a grateful face. "Goodbye, Meggy, I hope the Kings won't strain today. Don't fret about Father, dear," she added, as they parted.

"And I hope Aunt March won't croak. Your hair is becoming, and it looks very boyish and nice," returned Meg, trying not to smile at the curly head, which looked comically small on her tall sister's shoulders.

"That's my only comfort." And, touching her hat a la Laurie, away went Jo, feeling like a shorn sheep on a wintry day.

News from their father comforted the

girls very much, for though dangerously ill, the presence of the best and tenderest of nurses had already done him good. Mr. Brooke sent a bulletin every day, and as the head of the family, Meg insisted on reading the dispatches, which grew more cheerful as the week passed. At first, everyone was eager to write, and plump envelopes were carefully poked into the letter box by one or other of the sisters, who felt rather important with their Washington correspondence. As one of these packets contained characteristic notes from the party, we will rob an imaginary mail, and read them.

My dearest Mother:

It is impossible to tell you how happy your last letter made us, for the news was so good we couldn't help laughing and crying over it. How very kind Mr. Brooke is, and how fortunate that Mr. Laurence's business detains him near you so long, since he is so useful to you and Father.

The girls are all as good as gold. Jo helps me with the sewing, and insists on doing all sorts of hard jobs. I should be afraid she might overdo, if I didn't know her 'moral fit' wouldn't last long. Beth is as regular about her tasks as a clock, and never forgets what you told her. She grieves about Father, and looks sober

except when she is
at her little piano.
Amy minds me nicely,
and I take great care
of her. She does her
own hair, and I am
teaching her to make
buttonholes and
mend her stockings.
She tries very hard,
and I know you will
be pleased with
her improvement
when you come. Mr.
Laurence watches
over us like a

motherly old hen, as Jo says, and Laurie is very kind and neighborly. He and Jo keep us merry, for we get pretty blue sometimes, and feel like orphans, with you so far away. Hannah is a perfect saint. She does not scold at all, and always calls me Miss Margaret, which is quite proper, you know, and treats me with respect.

We are all well and busy, but we long, day and night, to have you back. Give my dearest love to Father, and believe me, ever your own...

MEG

This note, prettily written on scented paper, was a great contrast to the next, which was scribbled on a big sheet of thin foreign paper, ornamented with blots and all manner of flourishes and curly-tailed letters.

My precious Marmee:

Three cheers for dear Father! Brooke was a trump to telegraph right off, and let us know the minute he was better. I rushed up garret when the letter came, and tried to thank god for being so good to us, but I could only cry, and say, "I'm glad! I'm glad!" Didn't that do as well as a regular prayer? For I felt a great many in my heart. We have such funny times, and now I can enjoy them, for everyone is so desperately good, it's like living in a nest of turtledoves. You'd laugh to see Meg head the table and try to be motherish. She gets prettier every day, and I'm in love with her sometimes. The children are regular archangels, and I—well, I'm Jo, and never shall be anything else. Oh, I must tell you that I came near having a quarrel with Laurie. I freed my mind about a silly little thing, and he was offended. I was right, but didn't speak as I ought, and he marched home, saying he wouldn't come again till I begged pardon. I declared I wouldn't and got mad. It lasted all day. I felt bad and wanted you very much. Laurie and I are both so proud, it's hard to beg pardon. But I thought he'd come to it, for I was in the right. He didn't come, and just at night I remembered what you said when Amy fell into the river. I read my little book, felt better, resolved not to let the sun set on my anger, and ran over to tell Laurie I was sorry. I met him at the gate, coming for the same thing. We both laughed, begged each other's pardon, and felt all good and comfortable again.

I made a 'pome' yesterday, when I was helping Hannah wash, and as Father likes my silly little things, I put it in to amuse him. Give him my lovingest hug that ever was, and kiss yourself a dozen times for your...

TOPSY-TURVY JO

A SONG FROM THE SUDS

Queen of my tub, I merrily sing,

While the white foam rises high,

And sturdily wash and rinse and wring,

And fasten the clothes to dry.

Then out in the free fresh air they swing,

Under the sunny sky.

I wish we could wash from our hearts and souls

The stains of the week away,

And let water and air by their magic make

Ourselves as pure as they.

Then on the earth there would be indeed,

A glorious washing day!

Along the path of a useful life,

Will heart's-ease ever bloom.

The busy mind has no time to think

Of sorrow or care or gloom.

And anxious thoughts may be swept away,

As we bravely wield a broom.

I am glad a task to

me is given,

To labor at day by day,

For it brings me health and strength and hope,

And I cheerfully learn to say,

"Head, you may think, Heart, you may feel,

But, Hand, you shall work alway!"

Dear Mother,
There is only room
for me to send my
love, and some
pressed pansies from
the root I have been
keeping safe in the
house for Father to
see. I read every
morning, try to be
good all day, and sing
myself to sleep with
Father's tune. I can't
sing 'LAND OF THE
LEAL' now, it makes
me cry. Everyone is

very kind, and we are as happy as we can be without you. Amy wants the rest of the page, so I must stop. I didn't forget to cover the holders, and I wind the clock and air the rooms every day.

Kiss dear Father on the cheek he calls mine. Oh, do come soon to your loving...

LITTLE BETH

Ma Chere Mamma,

We are all well I do
my lessons always
and never corroberate
the girls—Meg says
I mean contradick so
I put in both words
and you can take the
properest. Meg is a
great comfort to me
and lets me have jelly
every night at tea
its so good for me Jo
says because it keeps
me sweet tempered.

Laurie is not as respeckful as he ought to be now I am almost in my teens, he calls me Chick and hurts my feelings by talking French to me very fast when I say Merci or Bon jour as Hattie King does. The sleeves of my blue dress were all worn out, and Meg put in new ones, but the full front came wrong and they are more blue than the dress. I felt bad but did not fret I bear my troubles well but I do wish Hannah would put more starch in my aprons and have buckwheats every day. Can't she? Didn't I make that interrigation point nice? Meg says my punchtuation and spelling are disgraceful and I am mortyfied but dear me I have so

many things to
do, I can't stop.
Adieu, I send heaps
of love to Papa.
Your affectionate
daughter...

AMY CURTIS MARCH

Dear Mis March,

I jes drop a line
to say we git on
fust rate. The girls
is clever and fly

round right smart. Miss Meg is going to make a proper good housekeeper. She hes the liking for it, and gits the hang of things surprisin quick. Jo doos beat all for goin ahead, but she don't stop to cal'k'late fust, and you never know where she's like to bring up. She done out a tub of clothes on Monday, but she starched 'em afore they was wrenched, and blued a pink calico dress till I thought I should a died a laughin. Beth is the best of little creeters, and a sight of help to me, bein so forehanded and dependable. She tries to learn everything, and really goes to market beyond her years, likewise keeps accounts, with my

help, quite wonderful.
We have got on
very economical so
fur. I don't let the
girls hev coffee
only once a week,
accordin to your
wish, and keep em
on plain wholesome
vittles. Amy does
well without frettin,
wearin her best
clothes and eatin
sweet stuff. Mr. Laurie
is as full of didoes
as usual, and turns

the house upside down frequent, but he heartens the girls, so I let em hev full swing. The old gentleman sends heaps of things, and is rather wearin, but means wal, and it aint my place to say nothin. My bread is riz, so no more at this time. I send my duty to Mr. March, and hope he's seen the last of his

Pewmonia.

Yours respectful,

Hannah Mullet

Head Nurse of Ward
No. 2,

All serene on the
Rappahannock,
troops in fine
condition, commisary
department well
conducted, the Home
Guard under Colonel

Teddy always on duty, Commander in Chief General Laurence reviews the army daily, Quartermaster Mullet keeps order in camp, and Major Lion does picket duty at night. A salute of twenty-four guns was fired on receipt of good news from Washington, and a dress parade took place at headquarters. Commander in chief sends best wishes, in which he is heartily joined by...

COLONEL TEDDY

Dear Madam:

The little girls are all well. Beth and my boy report daily. Hannah is a model servant,

and guards pretty
Meg like a dragon.
Glad the fine weather
holds. Pray make
Brooke useful, and
draw on me for funds
if expenses exceed
your estimate. Don't
let your husband
want anything. Thank
God he is mending.

Your sincere friend
and servant,
JAMES LAURENCE

CHAPTER SEVENTEEN

LITTLE FAITHFUL

For a week the amount of virtue in the old house would have supplied the neighborhood. It was really amazing, for everyone seemed in a heavenly frame of mind, and self-denial was all the fashion. Relieved of their first anxiety about their father, the girls insensibly relaxed their praiseworthy efforts a little, and began to fall back into old ways. They did not forget their motto, but hoping and keeping busy seemed to grow easier, and after such tremendous exertions, they felt that Endeavor deserved a holiday, and gave it a good many.

Jo caught a bad cold through neglect to cover the shorn head enough, and was ordered to stay at home till she was better, for Aunt March didn't like to hear people read with colds in their heads. Jo liked this, and after an energetic rummage from garret to cellar, subsided on the sofa to nurse her cold with arsenicum and books. Amy found that housework and art did not go well together, and returned to her mud pies. Meg went daily to her pupils, and sewed, or thought she did, at home, but much time was spent in writing long letters to her mother, or reading the Washington dispatches over and over. Beth kept on, with only slight relapses into idleness or grieving.

All the little duties were faithfully done each day, and many of her sisters' also, for they were forgetful, and the house seemed like a clock whose pendulum was gone a-visiting. When her heart got heavy with longings for Mother or fears for Father, she went away into a certain closet, hid her face in the folds of a dear old gown, and made her little moan and prayed her little prayer quietly by herself. Nobody knew what cheered her up after a sober fit, but everyone felt how sweet and helpful Beth was, and fell into a way of going to her for comfort or advice in their small affairs.

All were unconscious that this experience was a test of character, and when the first excitement was over, felt that they had done well and deserved praise. So they did, but their mistake was in ceasing to do well, and they learned this lesson through much anxiety and regret.

"Meg, I wish you'd go and see the Hummels. You know Mother told us not to forget them." said Beth, ten days after Mrs. March's departure.

"I'm too tired to go this afternoon," replied Meg, rocking comfortably as she sewed.

"Can't you, Jo?"

asked Beth.

"Too stormy for me with my cold."

"I thought it was almost well."

"It's well enough for me to go out with Laurie, but not well enough to go to the Hummels'," said Jo, laughing, but looking a little ashamed of her inconsistency.

"Why don't you go yourself?" asked Meg.

"I have been every day, but the baby is sick, and I don't know what to do for it. Mrs. Hummel goes away to work, and Lottchen takes care of it. But it gets sicker and sicker, and I think you or Hannah ought to go."

Beth spoke earnestly, and Meg promised

she would go
tomorrow.

"Ask Hannah for some
nice little mess, and
take it round, Beth,
the air will do you
good," said Jo, adding
apologetically, "I'd go
but I want to finish
my writing."

"My head aches and
I'm tired, so I thought
maybe some of you
would go," said Beth.

"Amy will be in presently, and she will run down for us," suggested Meg.

So Beth lay down on the sofa, the others returned to their work, and the Hummels were forgotten. An hour passed. Amy did not come, Meg went to her room to try on a new dress, Jo was absorbed in her story,

and Hannah was
sound asleep before
the kitchen fire, when
Beth quietly put on
her hood, filled her
basket with odds and
ends for the poor
children, and went out
into the chilly air with
a heavy head and a
grieved look in her
patient eyes. It was
late when she came
back, and no one saw
her creep upstairs
and shut herself into

her mother's room. Half an hour after, Jo went to 'Mother's closet' for something, and there found little Beth sitting on the medicine chest, looking very grave, with red eyes and a camphor bottle in her hand.

"Christopher Columbus! What's the matter?" cried Jo, as Beth put out her hand as if to warn her off, and asked quickly. . .

"You've had the scarlet fever, haven't you?"

"Years ago, when Meg did. Why?"

"Then I'll tell you. Oh, Jo, the baby's dead!"

"What baby?"

"Mrs. Hummel's. It died in my lap before she got home," cried

Beth with a sob.

"My poor dear, how dreadful for you! I ought to have gone," said Jo, taking her sister in her arms as she sat down in her mother's big chair, with a remorseful face.

"It wasn't dreadful, Jo, only so sad! I saw in a minute it was sicker, but Lottchen said her mother had gone for a doctor, so I took Baby and let Lotty rest. It seemed asleep, but all of a sudden if gave a little cry and trembled, and then lay very still. I tried to warm its feet, and Lotty gave it some milk, but it didn't stir, and I knew it was dead."

"Don't cry, dear! What did you do?"

"I just sat and held

it softly till Mrs. Hummel came with the doctor. He said it was dead, and looked at Heinrich and Minna, who have sore throats. 'Scarlet fever, ma'am. Ought to have called me before,' he said crossly. Mrs. Hummel told him she was poor, and had tried to cure baby herself, but now it was too late, and she could only ask him to help the others and trust to charity for his pay. He smiled then, and was kinder, but it was very sad, and I cried with them till he turned round all of a sudden, and told me to go home and take belladonna right away, or I'd have the fever."

"No, you won't!" cried Jo, hugging her close, with a frightened look. "Oh, Beth, if you should be sick I never could forgive myself! What shall we do?"

"Don't be frightened, I guess I shan't have it badly. I looked in Mother's book, and saw that it begins with headache, sore throat, and queer feelings like mine, so I did take some belladonna, and I feel better," said Beth, laying her cold hands on her hot forehead and trying to look well.

"If Mother was only at home!" exclaimed Jo, seizing the book, and feeling that Washington was an immense way off. She read a page, looked at Beth, felt her head, peeped into her throat, and then said gravely, "You've been over the baby every day for more than a week, and among the others who are going to have it, so I'm afraid you are going to have it, Beth. I'll call Hannah, she knows all about sickness."

"Don't let Amy come. She never had it, and I should hate to give it to her. Can't you and Meg have it over again?" asked Beth, anxiously.

"I guess not. Don't care if I do. Serve me right, selfish pig, to let you go, and stay writing rubbish myself!" muttered Jo, as she went to consult Hannah.

The good soul was wide awake in a minute, and took the lead at once, assuring that there was no need to worry; every one had scarlet fever, and if rightly treated, nobody died, all of which Jo believed, and felt much relieved as they went up to call Meg.

"Now I'll tell you what we'll do," said Hannah, when she had examined and questioned Beth, "we will have Dr. Bangs, just to take a look at you, dear, and see that we start right. Then we'll send Amy off to Aunt March's for a spell, to keep her out of harm's way, and one of you girls can stay at home and amuse Beth for a day or two."

"I shall stay, of course, I'm oldest," began Meg, looking anxious and self-reproachful.

"I shall, because it's my fault she is sick. I told Mother I'd do the errands, and I haven't," said Jo decidedly.

"Which will you have, Beth? There ain't no need of but one," aid Hannah.

"Jo, please." And Beth leaned her head against her sister

with a contented look, which effectually settled that point.

"I'll go and tell Amy," said Meg, feeling a little hurt, yet rather relieved on the whole, for she did not like nursing, and Jo did.

Amy rebelled outright, and passionately declared that she had rather have the fever than go to Aunt March.

Meg reasoned, pleaded, and commanded, all in vain. Amy protested that she would not go, and Meg left her in despair to ask Hannah what should be done. Before she came back, Laurie walked into the parlor to find Amy sobbing, with her head in the sofa cushions. She told her story, expecting to be consoled, but Laurie only put his hands in his pockets and walked about the room, whistling softly, as he knit his brows in deep thought. Presently he sat down beside her, and said, in his most wheedlesome tone, "Now be a sensible little woman, and do as they say. No, don't cry, but hear what a jolly plan I've got. You go to Aunt March's, and I'll come and take you out every day, driving or walking, and we'll have capital times. Won't that be better than moping here?"

"I don't wish to be sent off as if I was in the way," began Amy, in an injured voice.

"Bless your heart, child, it's to keep you well. You don't want to be sick, do you?"

"No, I'm sure I don't, but I dare say I shall be, for I've been with Beth all the time."

"That's the very reason you ought to go away at once, so that you may escape it. Change of air and care will keep you well, I dare say, or if it does not entirely, you will have the fever more lightly. I advise you to be off as soon as you can, for scarlet fever is no joke, miss."

"But it's dull at Aunt March's, and she is so cross," said Amy, looking rather frightened.

"It won't be dull with me popping in every day to tell you how Beth is, and take you out gallivanting. The old lady likes me, and I'll be as sweet as possible to her, so she won't peck at us, whatever we do."

"Will you take me out in the trotting wagon with Puck?"

"On my honor as a gentleman."

"And come every single day?"

"See if I don't!"

"And bring me back

the minute Beth is well?"

"The identical minute."

"And go to the theater, truly?"

"A dozen theaters, if we may."

"Well—I guess I will," said Amy slowly.

"Good girl! Call Meg, and tell her you'll give in," said Laurie, with an approving pat, which annoyed Amy more than the 'giving in'.

Meg and Jo came running down to behold the miracle which had been wrought, and Amy, feeling very precious and self-sacrificing, promised to go, if the doctor said Beth was going to be ill.

"How is the little

dear?" asked Laurie, for Beth was his especial pet, and he felt more anxious about her than he liked to show.

"She is lying down on Mother's bed, and feels better. The baby's death troubled her, but I dare say she has only got cold. Hannah says she thinks so, but she looks worried, and that makes me fidgety," answered Meg.

"What a trying world it is!" said Jo, rumpling up her hair in a fretful way. "No sooner do we get out of one trouble than down comes another. There doesn't seem to be anything to hold on to when Mother's gone, so I'm all at sea."

"Well, don't make a porcupine of yourself, it isn't becoming. Settle your wig, Jo, and tell me if I shall telegraph to your mother, or do anything?" asked Laurie, who never had been reconciled to the loss of his friend's one beauty.

"That is what troubles me," said Meg. "I think we

ought to tell her if Beth is really ill, but Hannah says we mustn't, for Mother can't leave Father, and it will only make them anxious. Beth won't be sick long, and Hannah knows just what to do, and Mother said we were to mind her, so I suppose we must, but it doesn't seem quite right to me."

"Hum, well, I can't say. Suppose you ask Grandfather after the doctor has been."

"We will. Jo, go and get Dr. Bangs at once," commanded Meg. "We can't decide anything till he has been."

"Stay where you are, Jo. I'm errand boy to this establishment," said Laurie, taking up his cap.

"I'm afraid you are busy," began Meg.

"No, I've done my lessons for the day."

"Do you study in vacation time?" asked Jo.

"I follow the good example my neighbors set me," was Laurie's answer, as he swung himself out of the room.

"I have great hopes for my boy," observed Jo, watching him fly over the fence with an approving smile.

"He does very well, for a boy," was Meg's somewhat ungracious answer, for the subject did not interest her.

Dr. Bangs came, said Beth had symptoms of the fever, but he

thought she would have it lightly, though he looked sober over the Hummel story. Amy was ordered off at once, and provided with something to ward off danger, she departed in great state, with Jo and Laurie as escort.

Aunt March received them with her usual hospitality.

"What do you want

now?" she asked, looking sharply over her spectacles, while the parrot, sitting on the back of her chair, called out...

"Go away. No boys allowed here."

Laurie retired to the window, and Jo told her story.

"No more than I expected, if you are allowed to go poking

about among poor folks. Amy can stay and make herself useful if she isn't sick, which I've no doubt she will be, looks like it now. Don't cry, child, it worries me to hear people sniff."

Amy was on the point of crying, but Laurie slyly pulled the parrot's tail, which caused Polly to utter an astonished croak and call out, "Bless my boots!" in such a funny way, that she laughed instead.

"What do you hear from your mother?" asked the old lady gruffly.

"Father is much better," replied Jo, trying to keep sober.

"Oh, is he? Well, that won't last long,

I fancy. March never had any stamina," was the cheerful reply.

"Ha, ha! Never say die, take a pinch of snuff, goodbye, goodbye!" squalled Polly, dancing on her perch, and clawing at the old lady's cap as Laurie tweaked him in the rear.

"Hold your tongue, you disrespectful old

bird! And, Jo, you'd better go at once. It isn't proper to be gadding about so late with a rattlepated boy like..."

"Hold your tongue, you disrespectful old bird!" cried Polly, tumbling off the chair with a bounce, and running to peck the 'rattlepated' boy, who was shaking with laughter at the last speech.

"I don't think I can bear it, but I'll try," thought Amy, as she was left alone with Aunt March.

"Get along, you fright!" screamed Polly, and at that rude speech Amy could not restrain a sniff.

CHAPTER EIGHTEEN

DARK DAYS

Beth did have the fever, and was much sicker than anyone but Hannah and the doctor suspected. The girls knew nothing about illness, and Mr. Laurence was not allowed to see her, so Hannah had everything her own way, and busy Dr. Bangs did his best, but left a good deal to the excellent nurse. Meg stayed at home, lest she should infect the Kings, and kept house, feeling very anxious and a little guilty when she wrote letters in which no mention was made of Beth's illness. She could not think it right to deceive her mother, but she had been bidden to mind Hannah, and Hannah wouldn't hear of 'Mrs. March bein' told, and worried just for sech a trifle.'

Jo devoted herself to Beth day and night, not a hard task, for Beth was very patient, and bore her pain uncomplainingly as long as she could control herself. But there came a time when during the fever fits she began to talk in a hoarse, broken voice, to play on the coverlet as if on her beloved little piano, and try to sing with a throat so swollen that there was no music left, a time when she did not know the familiar faces around her, but addressed them by wrong names, and called imploringly for her mother. Then Jo grew frightened, Meg begged to be allowed to write the truth, and even Hannah said she 'would think of it, though there was no danger yet'. A letter from Washington added to their trouble, for Mr. March had had a relapse, and could not think of coming home for a long while.

How dark the days seemed now, how

sad and lonely the house, and how heavy were the hearts of the sisters as they worked and waited, while the shadow of death hovered over the once happy home. Then it was that Margaret, sitting alone with tears dropping often on her work, felt how rich she had been in things more precious than any luxuries

money could buy—
in love, protection,
peace, and health,
the real blessings
of life. Then it was
that Jo, living in
the darkened room,
with that suffering
little sister always
before her eyes
and that pathetic
voice sounding in
her ears, learned
to see the beauty
and the sweetness
of Beth's nature, to

feel how deep and tender a place she filled in all hearts, and to acknowledge the worth of Beth's unselfish ambition to live for others, and make home happy by that exercise of those simple virtues which all may possess, and which all should love and value more than talent, wealth, or beauty. And Amy, in her exile, longed eagerly to be at home, that she might work for Beth, feeling now that no service would be hard or irksome, and remembering, with regretful grief, how many neglected tasks those willing hands had done for her. Laurie haunted the house like a restless ghost, and Mr. Laurence locked the grand piano, because he could not bear to be reminded of the young neighbor who used to make the twilight pleasant for him. Everyone missed Beth. The milkman, baker, grocer, and butcher inquired how she did, poor Mrs. Hummel came to beg pardon for her thoughtlessness and to get a shroud for Minna, the neighbors sent all sorts of comforts and good wishes, and even those who knew her best were surprised to find how many friends shy little Beth had made.

Meanwhile she lay on her bed with old Joanna at her side, for even in her wanderings she did not forget her forlorn protege. She longed for her cats, but

would not have them
brought, lest they
should get sick, and
in her quiet hours she
was full of anxiety
about Jo. She sent
loving messages to
Amy, bade them tell
her mother that she
would write soon,
and often begged
for pencil and paper
to try to say a
word, that Father
might not think
she had neglected

him. But soon even these intervals of consciousness ended, and she lay hour after hour, tossing to and fro, with incoherent words on her lips, or sank into a heavy sleep which brought her no refreshment. Dr. Bangs came twice a day, Hannah sat up at night, Meg kept a telegram in her desk all ready to send off

at any minute, and
Jo never stirred from
Beth's side.

The first of December
was a wintry day
indeed to them, for a
bitter wind blew, snow
fell fast, and the year
seemed getting ready
for its death. When
Dr. Bangs came that
morning, he looked
long at Beth, held the
hot hand in both his
own for a minute, and

laid it gently down, saying, in a low voice to Hannah, "If Mrs. March can leave her husband she'd better be sent for."

Hannah nodded without speaking, for her lips twitched nervously, Meg dropped down into a chair as the strength seemed to go out of her limbs at the sound of those words, and Jo, standing with a pale face for a minute, ran to the parlor, snatched up the telegram, and throwing on her things, rushed out into the storm. She was soon back, and while noiselessly taking off her cloak, Laurie came in with a letter, saying that Mr. March was mending again. Jo read it thankfully, but the heavy weight did not seem lifted off her heart, and her face was so full of misery that Laurie asked quickly, "What is it? Is Beth worse?"

"I've sent for Mother," said Jo, tugging at her rubber boots with a tragic expression.

"Good for you, Jo! Did you do it on your

own responsibility?" asked Laurie, as he seated her in the hall chair and took off the rebellious boots, seeing how her hands shook.

"No. The doctor told us to."

"Oh, Jo, it's not so bad as that?" cried Laurie, with a startled face.

"Yes, it is. She

doesn't know us, she doesn't even talk about the flocks of green doves, as she calls the vine leaves on the wall. She doesn't look like my Beth, and there's nobody to help us bear it. Mother and father both gone, and God seems so far away I can't find Him."

As the tears

streamed fast down poor Jo's cheeks, she stretched out her hand in a helpless sort of way, as if groping in the dark, and Laurie took it in his, whispering as well as he could with a lump in his throat, "I'm here. Hold on to me, Jo, dear!"

She could not speak, but she did 'hold on', and the warm grasp of the friendly human hand comforted her sore heart, and seemed to lead her nearer to the Divine arm which alone could uphold her in her trouble.

Laurie longed to say something tender and comfortable, but no fitting words came to him, so he stood silent, gently stroking her bent head as her

mother used to do.
It was the best thing
he could have done,
far more soothing
than the most
eloquent words, for
Jo felt the unspoken
sympathy, and in the
silence learned the
sweet solace which
affection administers
to sorrow. Soon she
dried the tears which
had relieved her,
and looked up with a
grateful face.

"Thank you, Teddy, I'm better now. I don't feel so forlorn, and will try to bear it if it comes."

"Keep hoping for the best, that will help you, Jo. Soon your mother will be here, and then everything will be all right."

"I'm so glad Father is better. Now she won't feel so bad about leaving him. Oh, me!

It does seem as if all the troubles came in a heap, and I got the heaviest part on my shoulders," sighed Jo, spreading her wet handkerchief over her knees to dry.

"Doesn't Meg pull fair?" asked Laurie, looking indignant.

"Oh, yes, she tries to, but she can't love Bethy as I do, and she won't miss her as I shall. Beth is my conscience, and I can't give her up. I can't! I can't!"

Down went Jo's face into the wet handkerchief, and she cried despairingly, for she had kept up bravely till now and never shed a tear. Laurie drew his hand across his eyes, but could not speak till he had subdued the choky feeling in his throat and steadied his lips. It might be unmanly, but he couldn't help it, and I am glad of it. Presently, as Jo's sobs quieted, he said hopefully, "I don't think she will die. She's so good, and we all love her so much, I don't believe God will take her away yet."

"The good and dear

people always do die," groaned Jo, but she stopped crying, for her friend's words cheered her up in spite of her own doubts and fears.

"Poor girl, you're worn out. It isn't like you to be forlorn. Stop a bit. I'll hearten you up in a jiffy."

Laurie went off two stairs at a time, and Jo laid her wearied head down on Beth's little brown hood, which no one had thought of moving from the table where she left it. It must have possessed some magic, for the submissive spirit of its gentle owner seemed to enter into Jo, and when Laurie came running down with a glass of wine, she took it with a smile, and said bravely, "I drink— Health to my Beth! You are a good doctor, Teddy, and such a comfortable friend. How can I ever pay you?" she added, as the wine refreshed her body, as the kind words had done her troubled mind.

"I'll send my bill, by-and-by, and tonight I'll give you something that will warm the cockles of your heart better than quarts of wine," said Laurie, beaming at her with a face of suppressed satisfaction at something.

"What is it?" cried Jo, forgetting her woes for a minute in her wonder.

"I telegraphed to your mother yesterday, and Brooke answered she'd come at once, and she'll be here tonight, and everything will be all right. Aren't you glad I did it?"

Laurie spoke very fast, and turned red and excited all in a minute, for he had kept his plot a secret, for fear of disappointing the girls or harming Beth. Jo grew quite white, flew out of her chair, and the moment he stopped speaking she electrified him by throwing her arms round his neck, and crying out, with a joyful cry, "Oh, Laurie! Oh, Mother! I am so glad!" She did not weep again, but laughed hysterically, and trembled and clung to her friend as if she was a little bewildered by the sudden news.

Laurie, though decidedly amazed, behaved with great presence of mind. He patted her back soothingly, and finding that she was recovering, followed it up by a bashful kiss or two, which brought Jo round at once. Holding on to the banisters, she put him gently away, saying breathlessly, "Oh, don't! I didn't mean to, it was dreadful of me, but you were such a dear to go and do it in spite of Hannah that I couldn't help flying at you. Tell me all about it, and don't give me wine again, it makes me act so."

"I don't mind," laughed Laurie, as he settled his tie. "Why, you see I got fidgety, and so did Grandpa. We thought Hannah was overdoing the authority business, and your mother ought to know. She'd never forgive us if Beth... Well, if anything happened, you know. So I got grandpa to say it was high time we did something, and off I pelted to the office yesterday, for the doctor looked sober, and Hannah most took my head off when I proposed a telegram. I never can bear to be 'lorded over', so that settled my mind, and I did it. Your mother will come, I know, and the late train is in at two A.M. I shall go for her, and you've only got to bottle up your rapture, and keep Beth quiet till that blessed lady gets here."

"Laurie, you're an angel! How shall I ever thank you?"

"Fly at me again. I rather liked it," said Laurie, looking mischievous, a thing he had not done for a fortnight.

"No, thank you. I'll do it by proxy, when your grandpa comes.

Don't tease, but go home and rest, for you'll be up half the night. Bless you, Teddy, bless you!"

Jo had backed into a corner, and as she finished her speech, she vanished precipitately into the kitchen, where she sat down upon a dresser and told the assembled cats that she was "happy, oh, so happy!" while Laurie departed, feeling that he had made a rather neat thing of it.

"That's the interferingest chap I ever see, but I forgive him and do hope Mrs. March is coming right away," said Hannah, with an air of relief, when Jo told the good news.

Meg had a quiet

rapture, and then brooded over the letter, while Jo set the sickroom in order, and Hannah "knocked up a couple of pies in case of company unexpected". A breath of fresh air seemed to blow through the house, and something better than sunshine brightened the quiet rooms. Everything appeared to feel the hopeful change. Beth's bird began to chirp again, and a half-blown rose was discovered on Amy's bush in the window. The fires seemed to burn with unusual cheeriness, and every time the girls met, their pale faces broke into smiles as they hugged one another, whispering encouragingly, "Mother's coming, dear! Mother's coming!" Every one rejoiced but Beth. She lay in that heavy stupor, alike unconscious of hope and joy, doubt and danger. It was a piteous sight, the once rosy face so changed and vacant, the once busy hands so weak and wasted, the once smiling lips quite dumb, and the once pretty, well-kept hair scattered rough and tangled on the pillow. All day she lay so, only rousing now and then to mutter, "Water!" with lips so parched they could hardly shape the word. All day Jo and Meg hovered over her, watching, waiting, hoping, and trusting in God and Mother, and all day the snow fell, the bitter wind raged, and the hours dragged slowly by. But night came at last, and every time the clock struck, the sisters, still sitting on either side of the bed, looked at each other with brightening eyes, for each hour brought help nearer. The doctor had been in to say that some change, for better or worse, would probably take place about midnight, at which time he would return.

Hannah, quite worn out, lay down on the sofa at the bed's foot and fell fast asleep, Mr. Laurence marched to and fro in the parlor, feeling that he would rather face a rebel battery than Mrs. March's countenance as she entered. Laurie lay on the rug, pretending to rest, but staring into the fire with the thoughtful look which made his black eyes beautifully soft and clear.

The girls never forgot that night, for no sleep came to them as they kept their watch, with that dreadful sense of powerlessness which comes to us in hours like those.

"If God spares Beth, I never will complain again," whispered Meg earnestly.

"If god spares Beth, I'll try to love and serve Him all my life," answered Jo, with equal fervor.

"I wish I had no heart, it aches so," sighed Meg, after a pause.

"If life is often as hard as this, I don't

see how we ever shall get through it," added her sister despondently.

Here the clock struck twelve, and both forgot themselves in watching Beth, for they fancied a change passed over her wan face. The house was still as death, and nothing but the wailing of the wind broke the deep hush.

Weary Hannah slept on, and no one but the sisters saw the pale shadow which seemed to fall upon the little bed. An hour went by, and nothing happened except Laurie's quiet departure for the station. Another hour, still no one came, and anxious fears of delay in the storm, or accidents by the way, or, worst of all, a great grief at Washington, haunted the girls.

It was past two, when Jo, who stood at the window thinking how dreary the world looked in its winding sheet of snow, heard a movement by the bed, and turning quickly, saw Meg kneeling before their mother's easy chair with her face hidden.

A dreadful fear passed coldly over Jo, as she thought, "Beth is dead, and Meg is afraid to tell me."

She was back at her post in an instant, and to her excited eyes a great change seemed to have taken place. The fever flush and the look of pain were gone, and the beloved little face looked so pale and peaceful in its utter repose that Jo felt no desire to weep or to lament. Leaning low over this dearest of her sisters, she kissed the damp forehead with her heart on her lips, and softly whispered, "Good-by, my Beth. Good-by!"

As if awaked by the

stir, Hannah started out of her sleep, hurried to the bed, looked at Beth, felt her hands, listened at her lips, and then, throwing her apron over her head, sat down to rock to and fro, exclaiming, under her breath, "The fever's turned, she's sleepin' nat'ral, her skin's damp, and she breathes easy. Praise be given! Oh, my goodness me!"

Before the girls could believe the happy truth, the doctor came to confirm it. He was a homely man, but they thought his face quite heavenly when he smiled and said, with a fatherly look at them, "Yes, my dears, I think the little girl will pull through this time. Keep the house quiet, let her sleep, and when she wakes, give her..."

What they were to give, neither heard, for both crept into the dark hall, and, sitting on the stairs, held each other close, rejoicing with hearts too full for words. When they went back to be kissed and cuddled by faithful Hannah, they found

Beth lying, as she used to do, with her cheek pillowed on her hand, the dreadful pallor gone, and breathing quietly, as if just fallen asleep.

"If Mother would only come now!" said Jo, as the winter night began to wane.

"See," said Meg, coming up with a white, half-opened rose, "I thought this would hardly be ready to lay in Beth's hand tomorrow if she—went away from us. But it has blossomed in the night, and now I mean to put it in my vase here, so that when the darling wakes, the first thing she sees will be the little rose, and Mother's face."

Never had the sun

risen so beautifully, and never had the world seemed so lovely as it did to the heavy eyes of Meg and Jo, as they looked out in the early morning, when their long, sad vigil was done.

"It looks like a fairy world," said Meg, smiling to herself, as she stood behind the curtain, watching the dazzling sight.

"Hark!" cried Jo, starting to her feet.

Yes, there was a sound of bells at the door below, a cry from Hannah, and then Laurie's voice saying in a joyful whisper, "Girls, she's come! She's come!"

CHAPTER NINETEEN

AMY'S WILL

While these things were happening at home, Amy was having hard times at Aunt March's. She felt her exile deeply, and for the first time in her life, realized how much she was beloved and petted at home. Aunt March never petted any one; she did not approve of it, but she meant to be kind, for the well-behaved little girl pleased her very much, and Aunt March had a soft place in her old heart for her nephew's children, though she didn't think it proper to confess it. She really did her best to make Amy happy, but, dear me, what mistakes she made. Some old people keep young at heart in spite of wrinkles and gray hairs, can sympathize with children's little cares and joys, make them feel at home, and can hide wise lessons under pleasant plays, giving and receiving friendship in the sweetest way. But Aunt March had not this gift, and she worried Amy very much with her rules

and orders, her prim
ways, and long, prosy
talks. Finding the
child more docile
and amiable than her
sister, the old lady
felt it her duty to
try and counteract,
as far as possible,
the bad effects of
home freedom and
indulgence. So she
took Amy by the
hand, and taught her
as she herself had
been taught sixty

years ago, a process which carried dismay to Amy's soul, and made her feel like a fly in the web of a very strict spider.

She had to wash the cups every morning, and polish up the old-fashioned spoons, the fat silver teapot, and the glasses till they shone. Then she must dust the room, and what a trying job that was. Not a speck escaped Aunt March's eye, and all the furniture had claw legs and much carving, which was never dusted to suit. Then Polly had to be fed, the lap dog combed, and a dozen trips upstairs and down to get things or deliver orders, for the old lady was very lame and seldom left her big chair. After these tiresome labors, she must do her lessons, which was a daily trial of every virtue she possessed. Then she was allowed one hour for exercise or play, and didn't she enjoy it?

Laurie came every day, and wheedled Aunt March till Amy was allowed to go out with him, when they walked and rode and had capital times. After dinner, she had to read aloud, and sit still while the old lady slept, which she usually did for an hour, as she dropped off over the first page. Then patchwork or towels appeared, and Amy sewed with outward meekness and inward rebellion till dusk, when she was allowed to amuse herself as she liked till teatime. The evenings were the worst of all, for Aunt March fell to telling long stories about her youth, which were so unutterably dull that Amy was always ready to go to bed, intending to cry over her hard fate, but usually going to sleep before she had squeezed out more than a tear or two.

If it had not been for Laurie, and old Esther, the maid, she felt that she never could have got through that dreadful time. The parrot alone was enough to drive her distracted, for he soon felt that she did not admire him, and revenged himself by being as mischievous as possible. He pulled her hair whenever

she came near him,
upset his bread and
milk to plague her
when she had newly
cleaned his cage,
made Mop bark
by pecking at him
while Madam dozed,
called her names
before company,
and behaved in all
respects like an
reprehensible old
bird. Then she could
not endure the dog, a
fat, cross beast who

snarled and yelped at her when she made his toilet, and who lay on his back with all his legs in the air and a most idiotic expression of countenance when he wanted something to eat, which was about a dozen times a day. The cook was bad-tempered, the old coachman was deaf, and Esther the only one who ever took any notice of the young lady.

Esther was a Frenchwoman, who had lived with 'Madame', as she called her mistress, for many years, and who rather tyrannized over the old lady, who could not get along without her. Her real name was Estelle, but Aunt March ordered her to change it,

and she obeyed, on
condition that she
was never asked to
change her religion.
She took a fancy to
Mademoiselle, and
amused her very
much with odd stories
of her life in France,
when Amy sat with
her while she got
up Madame's laces.
She also allowed her
to roam about the
great house, and
examine the curious

and pretty things stored away in the big wardrobes and the ancient chests, for Aunt March hoarded like a magpie. Amy's chief delight was an Indian cabinet, full of queer drawers, little pigeonholes, and secret places, in which were kept all sorts of ornaments, some precious, some merely curious, all more or less antique. To examine and arrange these things gave Amy great satisfaction, especially the jewel cases, in which on velvet cushions reposed the ornaments which had adorned a belle forty years ago. There was the garnet set which Aunt March wore when she came out, the pearls her father gave her on her wedding day, her lover's diamonds, the jet mourning rings and pins, the queer lockets, with portraits of dead friends and weeping willows made of hair inside, the baby bracelets her one little daughter had worn, Uncle March's big watch, with the red seal so many childish hands had played with, and in a box all by itself lay Aunt March's wedding ring, too small now for her fat finger, but put carefully away like the most precious jewel of them all.

"Which would Mademoiselle choose if she had her will?" asked Esther, who always sat near to watch over and lock up the valuables.

"I like the diamonds

best, but there is no necklace among them, and I'm fond of necklaces, they are so becoming. I should choose this if I might," replied Amy, looking with great admiration at a string of gold and ebony beads from which hung a heavy cross of the same.

"I, too, covet that, but not as a necklace.

Ah, no! To me it is a rosary, and as such I should use it like a good catholic," said Esther, eyeing the handsome thing wistfully.

"Is it meant to use as you use the string of good-smelling wooden beads hanging over your glass?" asked Amy.

"Truly, yes, to pray with. It would be

pleasing to the saints if one used so fine a rosary as this, instead of wearing it as a vain bijou."

"You seem to take a great deal of comfort in your prayers, Esther, and always come down looking quiet and satisfied. I wish I could."

"If Mademoiselle was a Catholic, she would find true comfort, but as that is not to be, it would be well if you went apart each day to meditate and pray, as did the good mistress whom I served before Madame. She had a little chapel, and in it found solacement for much trouble."

"Would it be right for me to do so too?" asked Amy, who in her loneliness felt the need of help of some sort, and found that she was apt to forget her little book, now that Beth was not there to remind her of it.

"It would be excellent and charming, and I shall gladly arrange the little dressing room for you if you like it. Say nothing to Madame, but when she sleeps go you and sit alone a while to think good thoughts, and pray the dear God preserve your sister."

Esther was truly pious, and quite sincere in her advice, for she had an affectionate heart, and felt much for the sisters in their anxiety. Amy liked the idea, and gave her leave to arrange the light closet next her room, hoping it would do her good.

"I wish I knew where all these pretty things would go when Aunt March dies," she said, as she slowly replaced the shining rosary and shut the jewel cases one by one.

"To you and your sisters. I know it, Madame confides in

me. I witnessed her will, and it is to be so," whispered Esther smiling.

"How nice! But I wish she'd let us have them now. Procrastination is not agreeable," observed Amy, taking a last look at the diamonds.

"It is too soon yet for the young ladies to wear these things. The first one who is

affianced will have
the pearls, Madame
has said it, and I have
a fancy that the little
turquoise ring will be
given to you when
you go, for Madame
approves your
good behavior and
charming manners."

"Do you think so?
Oh, I'll be a lamb, if
I can only have that
lovely ring! It's ever
so much prettier than

Kitty Bryant's. I do like Aunt March after all." And Amy tried on the blue ring with a delighted face and a firm resolve to earn it.

From that day she was a model of obedience, and the old lady complacently admired the success of her training. Esther fitted up the closet with a

little table, placed a
footstool before it,
and over it a picture
taken from one of
the shut-up rooms.
She thought it was of
no great value, but,
being appropriate,
she borrowed it, well
knowing that Madame
would never know
it, nor care if she
did. It was, however,
a very valuable
copy of one of the
famous pictures of

the world, and Amy's beauty-loving eyes were never tired of looking up at the sweet face of the Divine Mother, while her tender thoughts of her own were busy at her heart. On the table she laid her little testament and hymnbook, kept a vase always full of the best flowers Laurie brought her, and came every day to 'sit alone' thinking good thoughts, and praying the dear God to preserve her sister. Esther had given her a rosary of black beads with a silver cross, but Amy hung it up and did not use it, feeling doubtful as to its fitness for Protestant prayers.

The little girl was very sincere in all

this, for being left alone outside the safe home nest, she felt the need of some kind hand to hold by so sorely that she instinctively turned to the strong and tender Friend, whose fatherly love most closely surrounds His little children. She missed her mother's help to understand and rule herself, but having been taught where to look, she did her best to find the way and walk in it confidingly. But, Amy was a young pilgrim, and just now her burden seemed very heavy. She tried to forget herself, to keep cheerful, and be satisfied with doing right, though no one saw or praised her for it. In her first effort at being very, very good, she decided to make her will, as Aunt March had done, so that if she did fall ill and die, her possessions might be justly and generously divided. It cost her a pang even to think of giving up the little treasures which in her eyes were as precious as the old lady's jewels.

During one of her play hours she wrote

out the important document as well as she could, with some help from Esther as to certain legal terms, and when the good-natured Frenchwoman had signed her name, Amy felt relieved and laid it by to show Laurie, whom she wanted as a second witness. As it was a rainy day, she went upstairs to amuse herself in one of the large chambers, and took Polly with her for company. In this room there was a wardrobe full of old-fashioned costumes with which Esther allowed her to play, and it was her favorite amusement to array herself in the faded brocades, and parade up and down before the long mirror, making stately curtsies, and sweeping her train about with a rustle which delighted her ears. So busy was she on this day that she did not hear Laurie's ring nor see his face peeping in at her as she gravely promenaded to and fro, flirting her fan and tossing her head, on which she wore a great pink turban, contrasting oddly with her blue brocade dress and yellow quilted petticoat. She was obliged to walk carefully, for she had on high-heeled shoes, and, as Laurie told Jo afterward, it was a comical sight to see her mince along in her gay suit, with Polly sidling and bridling just behind her, imitating her as well as he could, and occasionally stopping to laugh or exclaim,

"Ain't we fine? Get along, you fright! Hold your tongue! Kiss me, dear! Ha! Ha!"

Having with difficulty restrained an explosion of merriment, lest it should offend her majesty, Laurie tapped and was graciously received.

"Sit down and rest while I put these things away, then I

want to consult you about a very serious matter," said Amy, when she had shown her splendor and driven Polly into a corner. "That bird is the trial of my life," she continued, removing the pink mountain from her head, while Laurie seated himself astride a chair.

"Yesterday, when

Aunt was asleep and
I was trying to be
as still as a mouse,
Polly began to squall
and flap about in
his cage, so I went
to let him out, and
found a big spider
there. I poked it
out, and it ran under
the bookcase. Polly
marched straight
after it, stooped
down and peeped
under the bookcase,
saying, in his funny

way, with a cock of his eye, 'Come out and take a walk, my dear.' I couldn't help laughing, which made Poll swear, and Aunt woke up and scolded us both."

"Did the spider accept the old fellow's invitation?" asked Laurie, yawning.

"Yes, out it came, and away ran Polly,

frightened to death, and scrambled up on Aunt's chair, calling out, 'Catch her! Catch her! Catch her!' as I chased the spider."

"That's a lie! Oh, lor!" cried the parrot, pecking at Laurie's toes.

"I'd wring your neck if you were mine, you old torment," cried Laurie, shaking his fist at the bird, who put his head on one side and gravely croaked, "Allyluyer! bless your buttons, dear!"

"Now I'm ready," said Amy, shutting the wardrobe and taking a piece of paper out of her pocket. "I want you to read that, please, and tell me if it is legal and right. I felt I ought to do it, for life is uncertain and I don't want any ill feeling over my tomb."

Laurie bit his lips, and turning a little from the pensive speaker, read the following document, with praiseworthy gravity, considering the spelling:

MY LAST WILL AND TESTIMENT

I, Amy Curtis March, being in my sane mind, go give and bequeethe all my earthly property—viz. to wit:—namely

To my father, my best pictures, sketches, maps, and works of art, including frames. Also my $100, to do what he likes with.

To my mother, all my clothes, except the blue apron with pockets—also my likeness, and my medal, with much love.

To my dear sister Margaret, I give my turkquoise ring (if I get it), also my green box with the doves on it, also my piece of real lace for her neck, and my sketch of her

as a memorial of her
'little girl'.

To Jo I leave my
breastpin, the one
mended with sealing
wax, also my bronze
inkstand—she lost
the cover—and my
most precious plaster
rabbit, because I am
sorry I burned up her
story.

To Beth (if she lives
after me) I give my
dolls and the little

bureau, my fan, my linen collars and my new slippers if she can wear them being thin when she gets well. And I herewith also leave her my regret that I ever made fun of old Joanna.

To my friend and neighbor Theodore Laurence I bequeethe my paper mashay portfolio, my clay model of a horse though he did say it hadn't any neck. Also in return for his great kindness in the hour of affliction any one of my artistic works he likes, Noter Dame is the best.

To our venerable benefactor Mr. Laurence I leave my purple box with a looking glass in the cover which will be nice for his pens and remind him of the departed girl who thanks him for his favors to her family, especially Beth.

I wish my favorite playmate Kitty Bryant to have the blue silk apron and my gold-bead ring with a kiss.

To Hannah I give the bandbox she wanted and all the patchwork

I leave hoping she 'will remember me, when it you see'.

And now having disposed of my most valuable property I hope all will be satisfied and not blame the dead. I forgive everyone, and trust we may all meet when the trump shall sound. Amen.

To this will and testiment I set my

hand and seal on this 20th day of Nov. Anni Domino 1861.

Amy Curtis March

Witnesses:

Estelle Valnor,
Theodore Laurence.

The last name was written in pencil, and Amy explained that he was to rewrite it in ink and seal it up for her properly.

"What put it into your head? Did anyone tell you about Beth's giving away her things?" asked Laurie soberly, as Amy laid a bit of red tape, with sealing wax, a taper, and a standish before him.

She explained and then asked anxiously, "What about Beth?"

"I'm sorry I spoke, but as I did, I'll tell you. She felt so ill one day that she told Jo she wanted to give her piano to Meg, her cats to you, and the poor old doll to Jo, who would love it for her sake. She was sorry she had so little to give, and left locks of hair to the rest of us, and her best love to Grandpa. She never thought of a will."

Laurie was signing and sealing as he spoke, and did not look up till a great tear dropped on the paper. Amy's face was full of trouble, but she only said, "Don't people put sort of postscripts to their wills, sometimes?"

"Yes, 'codicils', they call them."

"Put one in mine

then, that I wish all my curls cut off, and given round to my friends. I forgot it, but I want it done though it will spoil my looks."

Laurie added it, smiling at Amy's last and greatest sacrifice. Then he amused her for an hour, and was much interested in all her trials. But when he came to go, Amy held him back to whisper with trembling lips, "Is there really any danger about Beth?"

"I'm afraid there is, but we must hope for the best, so don't cry, dear." And Laurie put his arm about her with a brotherly gesture which was very comforting.

When he had gone, she went to her

little chapel, and
sitting in the twilight,
prayed for Beth,
with streaming tears
and an aching heart,
feeling that a million
turquoise rings would
not console her for
the loss of her gentle
little sister.

ABOUT THE AUTHOR

Louisa May Alcott grew up in New England with her three sisters, surrounded by famous Transcendentalists like Emerson and Thoreau. She worked to support her family, as a teacher, nanny, seamstress, and writer from a young age. She challenged gender norms of the time in many ways, including by being a lifelong avid runner.

ABOUT THE COVER

The image on the cover is adapted from a 1913 painting by Nikolai Astrup called "Summer and Playing Children."

THE STORY CONTINUES IN VOLUME 5

MORE BOOKS AT:

superlargeprint.com

KEEP ON READING!

This book is set in a font designed by Abelardo Gonzalez called OpenDyslexic

ISBN 9781093534313

Made in the USA
Monee, IL
23 January 2022

89702936R00193